A RUIN OF SHADOWS

A RUIN OF SHADOWS

L.D. LEWIS

Dancing Star
Press

This is a work of fiction. Names, characters, organizations, places, events, and incidents are either products of the author's imagination or are used fictitiously.

A Ruin of Shadows by L.D. Lewis

First published by Dancing Star Press: April 2018

Dancing Star Press
1222 N Grand River Ave
Lansing, MI 48906

w.ww.dancingstarpress.com

Cover Illustration by Emily Cheeseman

ISBN: 978-1-7321418-0-3

10 9 8 7 6 5 4 3 2 1

Printed in The United States of America

For Athena

General Édo stood on the bow of the *Nimbo Preto* beneath black sails, staring east in the night toward home. She enjoyed the glow kissed by moonlight into her deep brown skin. The stench of blood and sweat and pine embers had embedded itself in her shirt for about the hundredth time and no amount of sea air would shake it loose. The flag of the Boorhian Empire billowed gently overhead, a black field surrounding a great circle of orange. It was supposed to be the world, but the thin black outlines of continents were barely visible on any scale; their boundaries were only theoretical to the Empire.

A roar of laughter behind her. The Boorhian Empire's Shadow Army—a band of gunners, steel wielders, and creative arsonists who bled other people for the State—spread themselves about the stern where they'd been able to see and bask in the burning coast of Bastiat up until about an hour ago when it disappeared over the horizon. The novelty, the thrill of conquest hadn't vanished on them yet. They hadn't been at it for thirty years.

She took a breath and tried to exhale the years weighing on her soul. It didn't work, so she headed toward the laughter and her quarters beyond it.

Shadow *Army*, one might think, is a bit of a misnomer. After all, there were only seven of them. That's more of a *team* or *cadre* number. They were dubbed an army because of the sweeping efficiency with which they did their jobs. The General was their matriarch.

The seven nameless Shadows snapped to attention as she descended the stairs. Three men, four women, all young enough to be her sons and daughters had she ever had the mind to have children. They bore themselves still as Boorhian stone, save for the smiles still playing on some of their lips. That was likely Daynja's corruptive influence.

"As you were," the General waved their freedom and they melted back into something more casual. "What's funny?"

"Three got Five with a rope. He thought it was a snake," said Six. She and Seven, the youngest Shadows, were twins and shared the same grin over it.

Three was the Shadows' lone bomber and that's what she'd proudly tell anyone who asked about the three missing fingers of her right hand. She'd been a brawler once, but there was rarely a need for it as an assassin. Turned out she had a good mind for explosives, too. She smirked as she retracted her fuse line with black-smudged fingertips into a bundle circling her forearm. Indeed a thin, oil-slick bit of rope-end lay lifeless between Five's feet. A couple of Five's daggers nailed it to the deck.

"You? Afraid of snakes?" The General raised an eyebrow.

"Not afraid, Xir. I just don't trust them." Five replied, snatching his blades from the wood.

"Yeah, no. He's afraid," Six deadpanned.

"He wouldn't shut up about some serpent following him on the continent." Daynja's first Shadow, One's baritone interjected from where he sat off to himself, reclined on a pile of rope and heavy chain with a cap down over his eyes.

"We tried to tell him ain't a snake been spotted on Bastiat since you took out A Víbora, Xir," said Two. She was the other elder Shadow and sat at a table made of planks over barrels, hammering the brass ends from her bullet casings to fit them as cuffs to her locs. She glanced up occasionally, still amused by her sibling assassins. Four, the other gunner, sat at the table with her, focused intensely on cleaning her own weapons.

"A Víbora? When was that, 30 years ago?" Five scoffed and then blushed in the firelight as everyone stared at him for implying the General was old. He snapped to attention and bowed at the waist. "Apologies, Xir."

"Thirty-four years." The General said coolly.

"I don't think I ever heard this story completely," said Six.

The story of A Víbora was one really only Daynja could tell because everyone else who'd been there was dead. Still, she liked listening to how far tales of her exploits spun out over the years. And she liked having Three tell them.

The bomber Shadow smiled and put her knife away. "See, when she was a kid," she started, "they sent General Édo to Bastiat with this crew to put down some zealots north of the rocky coast. And while they're camped, the crew's attacked by swarms of serpents. One even bites the General, and she rips it out of her arm with its teeth still under her skin. She's the only one who doesn't die."

Six and Seven eyed the General as she showed them the scar tissue in her forearm, the teeth still distinct and embedded beneath it.

"Where was the mask?" asked Seven. That was always everyone's question. The General had come to Citadela as a child with this enchanted black mask that spawned an impenetrable armor over her entire body when worn. It had a fandom all its own.

"I was asleep. No time to put it on," said the General.

"So this snake's bitten her and she's poisoned and punchy and still hacking snake heads off with machetes. The remaining snakes flee," said Three, clearly excited. Fuse line coated her forearms in black grease as she gestured through the story. "She leaves the crew. They're dead anyway. For a day and a night she follows these snakes back north of the rocky coast to this cave with pits just full to fuck with vipers. Apologies, Xir."

"It was a quarry." The General almost laughed.

"Yeah? Alright, a quarry." Three shrugged. "Pits fifty meters long, filled to the tits with squirming, writhing, eat-your-face snakes, right? And who's at the center of all of it?"

From all their corners, the Shadows who'd heard this story before muttered, "A Víbora" dramatically with chuckles and snorts of laughter.

"A Víbora." Three grinned. "Twice as tall as One over there and pale as ash. He's a snake lord, and one of the Os Vazios legends. By the time Édo's there, she's tired and mad and her armor's not working well enough to cross a viper pit without dying half a dozen times. So she torches it."

"Torches it." Five echoed, shaking his head.

Six and Seven exchanged impressed nods.

"You'd think it'd be something elaborate, right? No. Just set the place on fire." Three kissed the fingertips of her left hand and made an exploding gesture. "Then she armored up long enough to cross the flames without getting burned just to cut him down with her own machete."

"My weapons arsenal wasn't nearly as refined back then." The General said.

"That was it?" asked Seven.

"More or less." The General shrugged. After that, she'd returned to Citadela with the gray, poisoned bodies of the crew and the head of her enemy. How they hadn't assumed she just killed them all herself was beyond her.

"It was unfortunate. I rather like snakes."

"That was your first kill for the Empire, Xir?" Six asked eagerly.

"First out of how many?" said Five.

"I don't keep count."

Even the busy Shadows stopped what they were doing to stare incredulously at her.

"You don't?" said Seven.

Daynja didn't know why she was surprised. "I just said I don't. You all do?"

"43," said Two.

"64. Give or take," Three smirked. "Bombs."

"40 even," One yawned.

Twenty-seven. Thirty-two. Thirty-one. Five was indignant about his paltry twelve.

Daynja's headache returned unexpectedly, but she gave her Shadows an impressed nod. "How thorough of you," she said.

"You've got to be in the hundreds by now, Xir." Two added as if the General was somehow in doubt about her prowess.

"Well, we will never know." The General stretched. "I am going to bed. Don't stay up too late. Drills at dawn."

The Shadows snapped to attention again and she put them at ease as she descended the stairs to her cabin.

After decades of dealing death at her own hands, how was it that her Shadows' glee in their jobs disturbed her now? Her glory days had been over for a while. In the beginning, there had been kings to kill. There'd been conquerings that required at least a little strategy and the use of her considerable wit. The war to turn back Os Vazios' colonization of Boorhia was over by the time she came to Citadela at thirteen. Her job had been to wipe them from the face of Irth by hunting down their legends and living gods. But all the big game was gone now and all that was left was the rabble, fledgling rebel clusters scattered across the continent with ideals toward growing and ridding themselves of Boorhia's suppression. All Daynja Édo was doing now was maintenance.

What she was now was tired. Tired or bored.

The last of the heat left in the room from a now-dead fire hit her as she entered her cabin and shut the door behind her.

Sixty-four?

"So I was thinking..." a voice mused unexpectedly. She spun to find a black youth—blue, by the moonlight—perched atop her desk by the one long window. She could make out the subtle glow of one gold eye as he watched her.

"Damn it, Djinni." She sighed at the umpteenth incarnation of the Artful Djinni and calmed the adrenaline in her blood.

"Yes, hello." The djinni replied cheerily. They'd been in the form of a leathery old woman when the General was a child, and any number of sentient things between then and now. Tonight, they were a dark, loc-haired kid in a galley boy's uniform, unfolding themself from the shadows and wondering at her with the twinkling gray and gold eyes that gave them away.

"How long have you been in here?" Daynja asked. She clicked up a lantern's light and dropped onto a small batik-print couch to scrawl numbers on the edge of an old sea chart.

43. 64—give or take...

"What time is it?" Djinni asked.

"Late." Daynja replied absently.

40. 32....

"I jest. Time is —"

"— is immaterial. Right. Got it." She finished for them. The djinni was a timeless, ancient creature. Not immortal, but too clever to die easily and they liked to throw that in her face regularly.

12. 27. 31.

Were there really over two hundred lives here?

The General wasn't a remorseful woman. In fact, she relished her Imperial Warlord title, and the magnificent tales spread of her particular brand of refined brutishness. Still, she frowned, tapping her pen in dots against the paper before dropping it entirely in favor of pouring herself a drink from the near-empty cachaça snifter on the table. Her famed mask lay idle and unremarkable beside it. The mask was plain, made of ebony with a gold ring through its septum and could probably do with a polish. It was a revered thing because as far as anyone knew, it was the source of all her power.

Far be it from her to correct them.

"All that immaterial time and you couldn't build a fire while you waited?" She sat back and swirled the white liquor in its mottled glass. A small burst of orange flame appeared before her in the fireplace.

The General smirked and got up to feed the fireplace from the neat stack of wood beside it.

"I was saying," Djinni continued, "We never vacation, you and I. Why do you think that is?"

Daynja scoffed. "What would you do on vacation that you don't do anyway?"

"The company makes all the difference." They winked and swung their legs over the desk. "So. If you were to, say, develop interests that had little to nothing to do with killing for the Empire, where in the world would you go to test them out?"

She rolled her eyes toward the engraved map of the world mounted over the fireplace. The Empire's territory was marked with dense, slanted hash lines and extended the entire massive Boorhian continent and some colonies in northeast Timber that were pleasant enough. The Bastiat continent Daynja was regularly charged with torching to some degree, was marked in less-dense hash lines. The Empire controlled it, of course. It couldn't be trusted to control itself. But it bore no Boorhian colonies because of the evil that always seemed to sprout from its soil.

"Everywhere is Boorhia," Daynja said. "Unless you're talking about South Timber which… interesting. But cold." She sipped her drink.

"Cold is what fires and furs are for," said Djinni.

Daynja's eyes wandered westward toward the specks of land beyond Bastiat. Eros was an archipelago leagues further from eastern Boorhia than any other nation. The islands themselves were united under Royal Saints, a king or queen who kept the nation's relationship to the Old Gods most of the world used to worship.

They were pacifists, so she had never had reason to go there. She imagined it was warm, quaint, and perfectly boring.

"Something else on your mind?" Djinni asked.

"Do you remember when we met?"

"When I met you or when you met me? In either case, yes."

"What did you think I'd end up doing with my life by now?"

"Oh I thought you'd be dead already," said Djinni. Their glibness sounded strange in a young boy's voice.

"That right?" Daynja blinked.

"When *I* met *you*, you were a very small creature cradled in the dust of your parents' bones. When *you* met *me*, you were taller and lacked the sense not to steal from me."

"I was *surviving* at ten and thought I was stealing from an old woman who could spare it."

"My point exactly. Your parents didn't live long enough to teach you not to underestimate mysterious old women. You were already repeating their mistakes at an impressively accelerated rate."

Daynja shrugged. Djinni had a point.

Djinni'd been there the day her vagabond parents conned a bitter old nun named Gigi who just so happened to know enough Old Magik to make them regret it. Daynja's mother was heavy with her at the time. Bearing no ill will to an unborn child, Gigi cursed the couple to accelerated age but blessed the child to be impervious. And so Daynja's once young and clever parents aged as many decades as years that passed until one morning, when she was five, she woke in the Vazios monastery ruins where they lived to find herself lying on the cobalt blue of her mother's dress. Her mother's bones had turned to ash within it as if she'd been dead a century already. Her father's lay beside her.

Djinni'd been there that day, too.

"What did *you* think you'd be doing?" They asked.

"When I was ten? I don't know. Career thief? Scam my way into something comfortable?"

"Well you might have pulled that off…"

"Djinni…"

"What I mean is, you've fared better than either of us imagined, haven't you?"

Daynja looked at the map on her wall and was surprised how many won battles she could recall over its surface. She wondered…

She picked up her pen again and began to count.

∴

From the western shore of the continent, Citadela was a day's driftcar ride into the heart of the jungle. High-speed magnetic throughways were cut into the sprawling bases of ancient kapok trees so the Empire's hovering commercial and military vehicles could careen toward destinations all over the continent without bothersome friction. The technology had only recently begun trickling down to civilians. Soon, Daynja imagined, more of the forests would be cross-cut with slick black veins and the constant, nauseating, ear-popping hum of two metallic tons zipping through magnetic relays at high speeds would become the music of the continent.

If there was any kindness in the universe, she'd be long dead by then.

Ruins dotted the jungle along their route. Gray stone remnants of Os Vazios missions and burnt, toppled statues of legends were slowly being consumed by the living forest. The war had only just ended by the time Edo was born but she knew the stories well. Os Vazios had been a skeletal gray people with an air of perpetual hunger about them. They'd swarmed the continent and had used their sickly visage to worm their way into cities as beggars. They'd brought a sickness with them; something to do with white flies, something only they could cure.

They'd built these stone missions to treat those they afflicted. But the sick emerged from their care dead-eyed, un-emotive, barely recognizable to their families. And Os Vazios grew healthier. Like parasites. Missions became temples where worship of foreign gods was exchanged for healing. Temples became targets for Boorhia's revenge. Targets became ruins. And Os Vazios were driven from the continent.

They put in at a transit station about a mile from Citadela's gates, and in an exchange that was never *not* bizarre, traded the driftcar for ceremonial black rhinos.

Every time the General and her Shadows returned to Citadela, it required a celebratory parading down the city's main avenue on the backs of armored rhinoceros. The premise was ridiculous, of course. She who would ride a damn rhino in a battle charge cared nothing for the intact state of her spine. But the tradition extended back centuries before Citadela became the center of the world, so here she was for the umpteenth time eating an apple and staring at the ass-end of Deus, her rhino being dressed in his stall.

"All right there, General? You look a little grim."

"Huh?" Daynja glanced up to see the old man who ran the rhino stables staring at her with his eyebrows raised and a half-eaten apple in his fist.

"This is just my face, Mr. Moreno," she said.

"I don't know," he chuckled and joined her on the wall. "Looks like the face of someone wondering about the life choices they made to be staring at the ass-end of a rhino."

"See that a lot here?"

"Mm-hmm." Mr. Moreno chuckled and tossed her an apple of her own. He wasn't all that old, really. Had her by about ten, fifteen years but melanin had kept his wrinkles fine and the labor had kept him firm. And he always seemed to be happy.

Good for him.

"Too long away from my bed." Daynja told him. It wasn't completely a lie.

"Well, maybe they'll let you sleep in it awhile this time. There can't be too many more baddies to send you out after." Mr. Moreno shrugged.

"You'd think that, right?" Daynja bit into her apple and reveled in its sweetness. Perhaps hunger had something to do with her ennui.

Deus was escorted from his stall. The attendants adorned him in plates of studded black metal marked with red clay circles. His horn and the tips of his ears were sheathed in mottled gold. He was twice Daynja's height and met her eyes with his own bored gaze. He huffed from his giant nostrils, making clouds of a layer of dust on stone path.

"I know," Daynja told him. She patted his face and held the apple in her mouth to hoist herself up the chain-link ladder to his saddle. Behind them, the other seven slightly smaller rhinos were being brought out from their dressing stalls in a line, their attendants standing back with bowed heads.

She blew a two-note whistle for her Shadows and called "Mount up!"

The Shadows appeared quickly from wherever they'd each been loitering during the wait. They aligned their animals in two columns behind One, who centered himself on her.

"Go on, Deus," she muttered, and the beast led the lot of them tromping onward toward the city.

Before the arrival of Os Vazios, Citadela was just another Boorhian nation-state that made for a spectacular sight. For miles the city sprawled across a valley south of the distant mountain line that split the continent between its lands of hot, lush greenery and cool, arid, nothingness.

After Os Vazios, the city sheltered refugees behind its walls and gates, and became the center for all of Boorhia's counter-offensive measures. An ocean of clay tile rooftops marked civilian territory. A cluster of tall, black buildings in the city's northern interior marked the military compound. The ministry that had once governed Citadela was now overseen by emperors, and the blood-orange glass dome dominating the city's center was no longer the capitol building, but a palace.

A few hundred yards out, Daynja chucked her apple stem into the tree line. A crooked-looking jacaranda marked the place just outside the visual range of anyone who cared to look outside the city's gate. She had used it for as long as she'd been doing this, to know when to pull the mask from her hip and wear it. Boorhia loved its legends, and the impenetrable General Édo was a favorite. She thought it rude to ruin the illusion with her mortal face.

She sighed, looking into the back of the mask for the thousandth time before placing it over her face. At once, the legendary black armor crept over her body, beginning with her eyes, and coating everything from hair follicle to toenail.

The General didn't have a personal god, nor did she know which of the existing ones were even canon anymore. But the start of the city was marked by alabaster obelisks with shallow cubbies carved in their faces for the placing of miniature wood or stone idols so regional gods and saints knew where to find and bless their faithful while they were visiting. Beyond them, two chimeric stone goddesses a hundred meters tall, stood armed on either side of the city's gate. There was no shortage of divine feminine architecture in Citadela.

The black gate opened as General Édo and the Shadows approached. Cheering crowds already lined the avenue. She didn't know how they knew to assemble because she was always on the other side of the gate when they did. The city still smelled of dew and morning coffee and prayer-burnt herbs. Petals and whole blossoms in every color were flung into the road before the rhinos. Their riders remained stoic, forward-looking, as if they were marble busts of themselves and not wholly revered flesh. Small children showed off paper and tree bark masks of their own and waved frantically to get the General's attention to flaunt them. By ten years of age, most of them would be small soldiers beginning their training on the other side of the inner gate.

The indulgent little procession ambled toward the inner gate to the military district at the far end of the avenue, where black-clad soldiers stood in solid lines and a team of advisors and lesser generals waited to welcome them back.

The inner gate —two obscenely tall and ornate iron doors— closed behind them, and the cheers dwindled to breezy sounds well over their heads. Deus groaned audibly as General Édo dismounted, equally relieved it was over and already dreading the next time it had to happen. The Shadows followed her lead and moved swiftly into a standing formation with the other soldiers. Pages saluted quickly and guided the rhinos away without much ceremony at all and Daynja heard and disregarded the congratulations from members of the military's old guard who didn't particularly like her but who were here because her life was still exceedingly more interesting than their own.

She'd been serious about missing her bed and turned to dismiss her Shadows.

"General Édo," called a familiar voice.

Édo's childhood mentor, the stout Mr. Remy, approached quickly. He was short with a feisty stride and always seemed ripe with a complaint.

Daynja took advantage of her mask's hiding the curses she muttered before she removed it and tucked it under her arm. The armor disappeared with it. The Shadows saluted.

"Good morning, Mr. Remy," she said, barely tempering her irritation. It wasn't that she didn't like or respect the man, but he was another ridiculous obstacle in a morning that was going on too long.

"Welcome back." He replied with a tight, compulsory smile. "I trust everything went as expected."

"Yes," she said flatly.

"Good. Emperor Negus has a request to make of you."

Daynja's skin prickled. She'd grown up with the Emperor and trained under his mother's permission. Somehow he'd interpreted her debt to the Empress as a debt to himself despite his overwhelming unworthiness.

"Of course he does. No rest for the wicked..." Daynja scoffed.

"*And*, General, he'd like to discuss it with you tonight in the War Room. The other generals are in agreement with you that Bastiat's been picked clean and it's time to re-evaluate where they are using your talents."

"'Bastiat's been picked clean?' The *world* has been picked clean, Mr. Remy. I should know. I'm the one doing the damn picking!"

Mr. Remy, stoic in the face of decades of Daynja's stubbornness, held up his hand to stop the frothing she'd begun to do. She growled herself to silence.

"Tonight. The War Room." He said calmly. "Get rest and remember yourself by then."

Daynja glared after him as he walked away. She knew he felt comfortable leaving her seething in silence because he knew she would come, despite her protest. Everyone did the bidding of the Empire.

The way they *are using* my *talents*. She sneered at the thought. In the beginning at least, it'd been she using them. But she was thirty-six years removed from the beginning. Somewhere, things had changed.

The military men loitering in the forecourt around her

—men who estimated themselves her peers and superiors—flinched and looked away as her eyes scanned over them.

"You heard him." She said, turning back to the Shadows. "Tonight. Keep to your regular duties until then."

The Shadows dismissed themselves quickly for the most part, save for a lingering stare from One. Daynja couldn't make out his expression —confusion, doubt, a daring *bitterness,* perhaps— but it piqued her curiosity and so she called him back.

"One."

He stopped in his stride and moved smoothly back to stony attention. One had been with her longest. He'd grown from a spindly child into a towering young man, broad-nosed, dark-skinned, and handsome. Nothing about him was delicate but his eyelashes and his temper.

"Something on your mind just now?" She asked. At times his deep, interested eyes sparkled with something like the ambition forbidden to the Empire's soldiers. Now they regarded their General carefully.

"No Xir. I am as tired as you are."

Lies were also forbidden the Empire's soldiers. But she'd chosen most of her Shadows for their forbidden qualities.

"Speak freely, One. And don't waste my time."

"The Emissary is an important man. The way you speak to him is unbecoming." He said sharply. There was a coolness about him, as if he knew he was right and the General was wrong no matter what she said next. A century of Boorhian custom backed him.

Daynja nodded and kept her amusement to herself. "I see," she said. "It's good that you revere him. But Mr. Remy and

I have known each other a long time and our relationship is complicated."

"Like our relationship with you?" said One.

A breeze passed between them. Daynja watched as he dampened the twinkle of his eyes, the way he always did when he was caught being human.

"Not *un*like it, no." She considered for a moment whether probing was worth the responses she might receive. "You are dismissed," she decided instead.

One turned on his heel and excused himself up a stone staircase and out of the square toward the barracks. The other Shadows had gone swift as whispers toward whatever would occupy them into the evening.

Daynja made her own way out of the shadow of towering administrative buildings and classrooms toward the sun-drenched parade grounds that divided the fortress. Drum beats resounded in her chest with an ancient rhythm when she reached the top of the stairs. The grounds were littered with small soldiers in neat rows and columns running disciplinary drills and marching formations to the sound of the drums. Flag drills raised and lowered in precision even to the rhythm of the echoes. The scent of sweat, the sounds of clashing metal and adolescent war cries rising from the training pits to the east drifted on the wind.

She made her way across the drill pads to the towering residential compound reserved for the heads of Boorhia's government. The building's base was formed of monumental stone columns shaped as women in varying poses and regal expressions. Their empty eyes saw both nothing and everything. They may have been goddesses once, now reduced to propping up the homes of mortal men.

She was beginning to see herself in them.

She'd lived in the same small apartment on the thirteenth floor of the center tower since clinching her first success with A Vibora. It was sparsely furnished with fine things commissioned from all over Boorhia. A coffee table cut from a great, felled tree somewhere in the eastern forests. Chairs with illustrated histories carved into their legs, sofas stuffed with black wool and upholstered in tough hides of northern beasts. Here and there, golden accents and trinkets from trips she'd accumulated and held onto less for nostalgia, and more for lack of something better to do with them.

The open shutters over the balcony let in sunlight to highlight the dust she disturbed by plopping herself onto the sofa.

Her boots came off with some effort and she thought vaguely about a bath but lay on her back and closed her eyes instead.

∴

"405." General Édo muttered into her cachaça glass. She leaned against her balcony window overlooking the nighttime lights of the capitol.

"What's that?" Djinni asked, stretched out on the couch behind her.

"My count," she sighed. "I added it up. Between myself and the seven Shadows I command, four hundred and five deaths have been served at the pleasure of the Boorhian Empire."

"You're very good at your job," Djinni offered.

Oh absolutely, the General smirked and pensively tapped a fingernail against her glass. "Just… seems high."

"You seem troubled," they remarked.

"Eh," the General waved with a noncommittal groan.

Djinni shot upright with a gasp and an impish grin.

"Daynja Édo, are you feeling *guilty*?" they scoffed, incredulous.

The General cut her eyes at the demon as they popped up to get a better look at her face there in the dark.

"The subtly knitted brow, the sheen of vague sadness dulling those eyes. The Imperial Warlord of Boorhia has four hundred and five regrets! How positively *human* of you," they chuckled, delighted apparently by this development.

"That will do, Djinni."

"And here I thought you were all *mask*! Well I, for one, am proud of you. But I imagine the War Council won't be pleased. What do you intend to do then? Retire?"

No.

No, once you reached a certain level in the Boorhian Army, you died on the field or not at all. And who said it was guilt she felt anyway?

A clock tower sounded nine across the city.

"You should go," she said, finishing off her glass. "I have an appointment."

"I was thinking I'd stick around. You can tell me how it goes."

"I'm thinking you won't."

"Oh come now," Djinni's voice dipped into its sinister tenor. The residence warmed by degrees and things as light as the bourbon bottle began to levitate by inches. "Who loves you more than I do?"

The General allowed her glass to float out of her hand. She watched the uniformed men cross the drill pad below to the War Room. No one, in fact, loved her as much as Djinni did.

"Out. Now," she ordered, eyeing her reflection and running her fingers through the short, silver coils of her hair.

"Suit yourself." They huffed like a disappointed child. The room cooled and the floating objects dropped with clatters and thuds. "Be seeing you."

She felt them gone like air through an open window.

The General peered up into the stern faces of the stone goddesses as she headed out.

The sky was its deepest possible blue, clear and flecked with constellations named for Boorhia's greatest, feared minds. She'd picked out a cluster of stars for herself to the west, away from the bulk of legends and the last to be conquered when the sun rose daily. She'd be damned if she hadn't earned them.

The dome of the War Room's rotunda stood out against the darkness like the hot, white arc of a third moon. The men before it met one another with laughter and claps on the back like old poker buddies and not armchair mass murderers. Though admittedly, some of them were both. She was the only active warrior ever present at these things.

She proceeded across the expanse as the head of the speared formation of her seven black-clad assassins.

The formation stopped just inside the great hall. "Wait here," she said, and the Shadows fell swiftly into a neat, statuesque row beside the doorway.

A static filled the atmosphere tonight. It piqued Édo's senses as she nodded at the passing officers and ministers who made up the Emperor's War Council. They eyed her, some with lascivious smiles. They enjoyed her exploits as much as any drunk enjoyed drinking, but she knew what they thought of her.

Mr. Remy approached quickly from the tall doors at the far end of the hallway, his clicking footfalls staccato in their rhythm on the marble floor.

"General Édo. Shadows." Mr. Remy called. The Shadows bowed in his direction as he came upon them.

"Good evening, Mr. Remy." The General replied.

He took stock of the Shadows, sizing them up with keen eyes. "His Eminence is about ready to begin."

"Of course he is. Let's get on with it."

"Bring your lieutenant," suggested Mr. Remy. How unorthodox. The General hesitated with a raised eyebrow and watched him for signs that he might explain why. "General, we haven't got all day."

"Join us, One," the General shrugged. One stepped forward and followed them into the chamber.

The War Council took seats at a senselessly large round table. Spectating officers and ministers stood against walls around them. The First Shadow took his place standing at the General's back.

"General Édo, and her First Shadow. How pleased we are you've been able to join us." Emperor Negus smiled politely on his gilded throne at the far end.

"Pleased as always to be here, Your Eminence," Daynja said flatly.

Negus's Chief Minister stood and called the meeting to order. His beard and the hair on his head were so soft, coiffed, and white, he almost looked friendly.

Dossiers were dispatched around the table. Daynja flipped through it to see a young woman photographed on a beach with a few dozen discontents. The buzzing began in her ears again. Something wrong was coming.

The Minister began, "We have received word that a Queen-Saint has ascended to the throne in Eros despite Emperor Negus's merciful suggestions that that not happen. With her comes the growth of certain anti-Empire rhetoric and a faction we'd like to be rid of."

"So, a show of force operation. Squash the rebels, remind them of their place. This is a militia job. The Shadows are overqualified." Daynja offered.

"Not quite, General," Emperor Negus interjected. "You and the Shadow Army will eliminate the Queen-Saint and her faction."

Here, the General laughed. The sound was said to shake souls free of the bones they clung to. Surrounded as she was by soulless men, however, there was nothing here to shake.

"You're joking," she scoffed at the Minister. "She's a child! And Eros is a pious island nation. They're pacifists because the Queen-Saint's main job is to beg favors from old, dead gods for their defense. There is absolutely no threat here."

The Minister glared and the Emperor's jaw clenched the way it did when the serenity General Édo's brutishness granted him was inconvenienced. The men on the edges of the room seethed, the shifts of their loosening bodies in their pristine uniforms audible in the silence of the rotunda.

"Am I to understand you're confused about these orders?" The Emperor spoke low in the hallowed oval, meaning to threaten her with his tone. She knew him too well to take him seriously.

"No," she smiled. "I'm quite clear. All the world I've put at your feet and this is what you'd do with it. What you'd have *me* do with it. I slaughter demons and demigods to make whatever point it is you are still trying to make about Os Vazios but this is beyond sense and *beneath* the Empire."

"You're out of line!" shrieked a reddening old Admiral along the wall, more paunch than punch now by the look of him.

"I was speaking to His Eminence," she said calmly.

"You forget your place, General," insisted the Chief Minister.

"With respect, Xir, it's more likely you've had my place mistaken."

In a rage, Negus stood to admonish his viciously insubordinate General likely in some blustering, stammered fashion, but she stood as well to take her leave. The sheer audacity left the warnings he was prepared to spew boiling in his throat.

"I'll be invoking Autonomy, Xir. His Eminence's prerogative is his own. But I will not allow myself to be a part of it this time. Excuse me." She bowed at the waist and turned to stride away toward the door.

"You have not been dismissed!" The Emperor bellowed, and men stepped between the General and the door with an urgent sort of smugness carved into their sagging faces. She exhaled slowly and turned back to his attention, plotting her escape with One at her back in case the need arose.

"Autonomy isn't for *you*. If it was, the time to take it would have been when you were too young to know better so Mr. Remy could have left your impertinent hide in the muck where he found you. You owe your every breath to the State. And you *will* pay that debt."

Debt? Oh my, she had words for that.

The General controlled the sneer threatening her lips. There were easily twenty men here, all old, yes, but it would be foolish to discount their decades of combat experience just because they'd gone a little thick round the middle. She smelled an eagerness on them. They wanted her to violently misstep. She felt the secret armor in her blood rising to the surface beneath the collar of her shirt.

This wasn't the time.

She relaxed into a smile but met the Emperor's pointed, imperious gaze. "Well, I tried."

"Then you'll brief the Shadows and report on a course of action within the week," said the Chief Minister. The rebellion squashed, he seemed comfortable again.

The General gave what could grudgingly be considered a nod.

"Now you may go," the Emperor declared with bass in his voice.

"Your Eminence. Ministers." She bowed for the second time and waited for the men barring the door to stand aside. Mr. Remy followed her and One into the hallway.

"What in the Three Known Worlds was *that*?" he blustered.

"Not now, old man."

"*Daynja Édo!*"

The General slowed her stride, cringing at the reflex that made her submit to this man's browbeating.

"What has gotten into you? You don't refuse him. It's unprecedented and will demand unprecedented consequences.

I guarantee as soon as you left they began trying to work around you."

"I said I'd comply."

"No, you didn't."

She stifled a groan and wondered if he would follow her all the way home.

"It's the mask, isn't it? The hubris of invincibility has finally addled your brain."

"Mr. Remy…"

"They've always said it should be kept in the armory, someplace we can regulate its use. But I've defended your keeping it, and…"

"MR. REMY."

"Then what is it?" He huffed.

She spun on him. "*I made him.* Negus's throne sits on corpses I delivered. I owe these men nothing. He will know that before the end."

Half a century of military bearing didn't allow Mr. Remy to flinch. He read her, looking up into her face the way he'd looked down into it thirty years ago.

"Whatever it is you're plotting, I'd advise against it," he said quietly.

"Who says I'm plotting anything?" Daynja started away again.

"I am your only friend in that room, General Édo." He called after her.

"And you should stop that when it stops serving you, Mr. Remy."

She whistled two sharp notes and her assassins fell into formation, trailing her out of the building.

"Are you plotting something, General?" wondered

One, his voice low as they marched back out into the moonlight.

"Only dinner, One," the General replied.

"You called Autonomy. If you don't intend to comply, you should give up the mask."

The General turned again on her army. One stared coolly down at her, while the others exchanged glances of confusion.

"Code of the Shadow Army." Édo growled. She made eye contact with all of them. "It means that you are Shadows. You originate from me and you do not exist without me. So you have no opinions unless I give them to you. You will have your orders when I create them. If that is clear, you are all dismissed."

Shadows Two through Seven went about their vanishing as ordered, but One remained rooted to his spot on the drill pad, standing at ease with his jaw clenched.

"Your boldness is both grating and poorly timed, One." Édo carped.

"We are forbidden egos," One insisted anyway. "Boorhian soldiers are born, trained, used here. And if we are exceptional, we are handed names so we can live forever as stars and stories. But you, General, you have never been one of us. We know you were this foreign, dirt-caked orphan in the Hinterlands when they found you. But you have always had a name and our fate is tied to yours. Your disgrace before the Emperor is *our* disgrace."

Daynja inspected him silently a moment, recalling the first image she'd had of him at nine or ten years old. His eyes were intense and intelligent, his slender, brown frame swift and graceful in its movements. Any steel weapon placed before him was wielded with effortless beauty and impeccable accuracy.

Why wouldn't he grow up to be trouble?

"I remember you all from before you were mine," she smiled slightly. "Your name, child, was Waahid. Do you feel any more powerful now, knowing that? Or are you still just the first of seven? Still of me, of Boorhia, and expendable at our whim?"

She waited for a response, for his lips to move as he fit his own lost name to them. He gave her nothing, just the stony gaze that meant he was thinking but didn't want to be caught doing it. She stepped toward him though, and found hints of confusion in his eyes. That would suffice.

"I know you must think you're exceptional, that your invitation into that room was for your *grooming* for something greater than what you are. And that may be the case. But I can guarantee you one thing tonight," she growled and leaned up into his face so close that barely air passed between them. "If you speak to me again without your sense, Waahid—*One*—I will flay you alive and feed you your own hide. Doubt me."

She left him alone on the drill pad with her promise. Every step away, she listened to the breeze for the blade she knew he would drive into her back. Eventually, she trusted, he would try.

∴

Daynja stood distracted on the catwalks overlooking the pits. It was her duty to the Empire that she continue to spend the daylight hours supervising training exercises and conducting inspections. Young soldiers grouped by age and ability sparred and practiced their formations in the grid of stone recesses on the east end of the fortress. Over decades, legions of men and women whose lives were pledged compulsorily and without question to the empire submitted under her gaze. They wanted her to make eye contact, to call on them for demonstrations so they might prove their value and be asked to join her Shadows.

Her boots crunched on the gravel over their heads as she moved about the grid. She remembered being a part of them. Not of them, but among them. She'd been a gangly, belligerent child, late to the game at thirteen and infected with ego. But she'd been recruited for her quick study and resourcefulness at the Empress's request to keep her out of trouble.

Men in uniform had once peered into the training pits to observe her. Their brass-loaded breasts made for annoyance in the sunlight. They gave voice to salacious and disquieting thoughts in whispers they didn't try hard enough to make inaudible while she sweat beneath them. They played intimidation games, staring into her eyes too long and too hard in order to break her concentration. It never worked because she neither knew nor cared who they were.

So when she watched the young soldiers, she left her brass at home. And when she made eye contact, it was only to push the ones who needed it.

She was more mindful today that they were children. The thought made the sun feel hotter and the sweat scorched her skin. Lately she'd been having dreams about the young queen she was supposed to kill and none of them were the victorious type. The hand she'd had in creating the force that would undo the child weighed on her. She had, in fact, been noticing more about the ground, for the new difficulty she found in holding her head high.

In her periphery, a young woman approached. She was pretty and wore the fortress's classroom uniform but had a bit too much of a twitch in her hips to be a soldier. A smile played about her lips, and as she drew nearer, she winked one gold and then one gray eye.

"Where have you been?" Daynja asked the Djinni.

"I've only been gone a minute," they replied, standing beside the General and joining her in feigning interest in the young soldiers below.

"It's been days."

"Possible," they shrugged. "Ti—"

"*Immaterial.* Yes."

"What happened? What did you do?"

"What do you mean what happened? Who says anything happened?" Daynja muttered and continued to pace the catwalk. Djinni followed.

"The words 'Autonomy', 'Édo', and 'traitorous demon' are floating around with unusual regularity and you're clearly in a mood. So this is either a very specific cosmic coincidence or you've done something."

Daynja sighed and watched the other officers milling about the area. Each did seem to be taking extra effort to keep their eyes from hers. "I expressed some… displeasure with a mission Negus proposed. Ordered. He wants me to kill the Eros queen."

"When are you leaving?"

She abruptly turned to Djinni and scowled. "She's a child!"

"She's a statesman!" Djinni scoffed. "What have you been doing this entire time but laying waste to creatures in her position?"

"This isn't the same. Os Vazios are a plague and I haven't minded clearing them. She's no threat to anyone. She is a *child*."

"They are children, too. You've helped make *them* into threats though, haven't you?" Djinni nodded toward the young soldiers clashing in the pits below. "This is about your 405 thing, isn't it?"

"Probably," she admitted. "What have you heard? The whispers?"

"There's talk of replacing you."

"Replacing me?" She raised an eyebrow.

"With your Shadow."

"One?" The other eyebrow raised itself. "I'll admit I get the sense lately that he's eager but he isn't *ready*."

"Doesn't have to be One. You do have six others. They're all pretty sure your job can be done as long as they have the mask."

"Is that right?" Daynja chewed the inside of her cheek and nodded down at proctors who waited for a sign of whether or not she approved of the exercises. How certain was she that all the rest of her Shadows wouldn't follow their brother's lead against her?

"You might consider that vacation more seriously now," Djinni chirped.

"I can't. I can't run off and let them kill that girl," Daynja insisted, though leaving sounded like an increasingly important thing to do.

"How do you intend to stop them?"

"Haven't figured that out yet."

"You're going to do something reckless."

"If I do, you'll show up to say something about it, won't you?"

"It'd be weird if I didn't."

A cluster of uniformed officers were coming toward them from the administrative buildings. She couldn't hear what they were saying, but two of them were the first men to look at her all day.

"You should go."

"You do realize I am a timeless being of incredible untold power and not actually someone who takes orders from you, right?" Djinni smirked. The General gave them a serious look and they relented, turning on their heel to head back wherever they'd come from.

The General squared her jaw as if bracing for something, an attack, another summoning from Remy or Negus. The uniformed officers met her gaze and saluted as they passed with no word but the conversation between them. She tried to relax but the sun was still too hot, the drums too loud. She couldn't keep herself from checking corners and the lines of rooftops for eyes sent to watch her. If Djinni was right and the chatter was now about replacing her, moves were already being made.

She smirked as she crossed the drill pad back toward her apartment. Thick jags of gold alloy filled widening cracks in the stone pathways she followed. They suggested to Daynja that the Boorhian Empire would always be able to repair whatever damage she inflicted in the name of saving the girl.

Unless, of course, she dismantled it entirely.

Her pulse quickened at the idea of conquering something

worthwhile for once. Emperor Negus would be dissuaded from the attack on Eros. And when he inevitably refused, he and anyone else who chose to be in the way of her mission would be removed with Daynja Édo's personal brand of violence.

Including One.

∴

Daynja still dreamed, just never the guilt-ridden nightmares expected of career murderers. If anything, her mind always returned to the ruins. She drifted off listening to her own breathing until the jungle sounds of her youth filled her mind, the drone of a million insects, leaves bothered by creeping things or distant breezes high overhead. The stars were always different through the holes in the thatched canopy her parents had built between crumbling pillars. She would lay where she could look through it. In her dreams she could almost feel her bony shoulders pressed against cold, gray stone, and smell heady jaboticaba and hearth.

Sometimes she heard her parents. Their voices were indistinguishable from one another in her memories by now. They were frail; each ages older than they'd been the day before, their faces gaunt shadows bickering in whispers near the cooking fire. She had never known them young or in the kind of love Djinni'd described. She knew them as two people surviving with one destiny, too proud to beg for what they were increasingly too weak to steal.

That was always the dream, little Daynja pretending to sleep beneath the canopy, watching her mother and father as living silhouettes before a crackling fire. Suddenly now though, she was lying on a mat of animal pelts with her head in her mother's lap. Her view was of her mother's bare feet at the bottom of a bright blue dress. They were dark and bony, nearly a century old, but clean. The toes tapped the air to some unheard rhythm. Ringed fingers with knuckles like knots ran the plaited rows of little Daynja's scalp. This was a memory.

"When will you die?" she heard herself say.

"When you forget me," her mother said. They had always spoken plainly of the curse.

"Will it happen to me?"

"Will what, meu amorzinho?"

"The Old Magik," she said. She looked up into her mother's face. It was long and thin, the cheekbones sharp and brown eyes over-large in her skull. She kept a gold stud in her nose, and when she laughed, her teeth were still intact and bright. It was not hard to imagine she was lovely once.

"No," her mother smiled. "Even magical crones have mercy for children."

Daynja jolted awake to find it was night and gooseflesh trailed her arms. She was alone. Bundles of braided razor-sharp fuse line called spiderwire lay scattered and unspooled across the coffee table where she dozed off and left it. She couldn't remember the last time she'd seen her mother's face in her dreams. Undoubtedly it had something to do with the Eros assignment.

"Caralho," she cursed quietly and drew a hand long over her face. She cursed again when she found her cachaça bottle had less than a finger left of the stuff in it. If she was going to sleep or find the creativity necessary to parse her plan, she would need to be lubricated. Outside her window, city lights still twinkled beyond the inner wall. Citadela was not asleep yet. There was still time to replenish her supply.

It wasn't expressly forbidden, but those who trained and worked within the inner walls rarely went out into the city. The romantic justification of course was that it was a distraction. Somehow engaging with the demilitarized world made one a weaker protector of it. That experience was sacrificed to make one a better soldier.

The practical reason was that everything a soldier of Boorhia needed was already inside the walls and if you were training hard enough, you were too tired to venture beyond what was convenient at the end of the day. What wasn't issued was requested and delivered by couriers. Meals were prepared by a small clutch of mediocre cooks and served and eaten in a dining hall at designated hours. It was mostly tough meat spiced beyond reason, an alternately watery or too-dry substrate, and an indistinguishable muddling of still more peppers and leafy greens. There was a library, a ball field, and enough down time and dark corners to sneak in clumsy, hormone-addled, adolescent trysts when needed.

She relished how quiet it was on base when the drums were stopped. So quiet, in fact, she could hear herself being followed. It was a faint, sporadic sound that trailed her through the inner gate; a jostling of cobblestone to her rear first on the left, then the right. Someone walking regularly would have produced the noise more consistently. This was someone who had to stop to hide and pace themselves behind their mark.

She donned a black straw farmer's hat — its wide brim useful in hiding her face as she walked the streets — and wondered who Negus had found brazen enough to tail her.

The General mainly came out for better food and hit the market stalls either early morning or late at night when the air was cool and the crowds were thin. She was a bit later than usual tonight. Flickering torch light still illuminated rooms in the tiered apartments of Citadela. Headlamps on humming driftcycles created disappearing pools of light on side roads as people returned home from late shifts. Her spy's footfalls were lost in the noise of the city but she still felt the eyes on her.

She watched the news of her arrival in the marketplace ripple through merchants on both sides of the street, manifesting in whispers and nods in her direction, the stoking of grill fires, the unpacking of vendors who'd just packed up for the night. Each declared something along the lines of "beautiful night, General" as she passed their stalls. She picked up a lime here, a bundle of wild cherries there, and pointed to what she wanted from grill merchants. Bits of tender boar and gator and whatever jungle beast was handy at the time made their way onto skewers with bright fruit and into grilled flat breads. The air was alive with smoke scented with citrus and burnt sugar.

Early in her career the vendors would protest, insisting she take the wares for free while she insisted on paying. What was the point of having money if she was not allowed to spend it? And then she let it be known that the back and forth of refusing her money was a waste of her very valuable time. Now they accepted the gold coins she pressed into their palms immediately, and kissed them as if they were blessings.

A stall at the far end of the marketplace opted for strings of etched iron and colorful glass lanterns instead of torch light. Daynja's cachaça vendor, an old woman with skin the color of clay and a hive of gray-white braids sat beneath them at the center of an assortment of cryptically marked jugs and glass bottles. She exhaled cigar smoke from dark lips and itched her nose with a tattooed finger. Her mountain of a grandson stood stone-faced in the background as a silent threat to the belligerent among the late-night drinking crowd.

"Beautiful night, General," she said in a voice that sounded like she gargled gravel. She didn't jump to her feet like anyone else might have. Her eyes were black and hard as diamonds and not at all impressed by the spectacle of General Edo. "Where you been?"

"The world's edge, of course," said Daynja. "And how are you, Margot?"

"I sell liquor. Business is always good so I am always good." Margot reached to a shelf behind her and brought forward a dark jug just small enough to carry without much effort. "I expected you sooner. You must have moved slower through the last bottle."

"Well, I just got back."

"Mm-hmm. Or you are getting old."

"What?" Daynja blinked.

"It happens." Margot shrugged. "You get old and you drink more or you drink less. No judgment here, girl."

Daynja considered a scathing reply, but none came to mind which, too, could have meant she was getting too old to be that petty. She placed her coins in Margot's outstretched hand and nodded a goodnight to her and her grandson before dropping the jug in her rucksack and heading back toward the gate. None but the merchants looked familiar so she turned her attention to the rooftops. If she'd been following someone here, that's where she'd be. And undoubtedly someone she once trained was doing the following now.

Cigar cherries dotted dark alleyways and rooftops washed white by the light of the Shattered Moon. Old friends gathered on high balconies to laugh over after-dinner drinks. Lullabies and lilting notes from plucked string instruments wafted out of open windows. No signs of anyone paying any attention to her.

A younger Daynja had imagined this mundanity would someday illustrate her life. She would rise from the gutter to earn normalcy, not move so impossibly far beyond it. Yet here she was, an aging apex assassin wearing a sunhat at night to avoid the adoration of people who had once avoided her.

An open-air tavern on one side of a four-way intersection hosted late shift tradesmen and visiting merchants who could afford to sleep in tomorrow. Tobacco smoke hung in a haze like the mists that crept in from the jungle at night. Loud, mingling conversations were punctuated by the slamming of heavy fists on hardwood tables in animated discourse or aggressive games of bones.

Daynja was peering through the crowd for anyone who might be too interested in her passing when gradually games stopped and drinks sloshed to stillness. Heads turned a few at a time toward shouts of "brother!" growing distant down a residential street. A male figure in a dark dishdasha moved away from them at a listless shuffle either not hearing or not heeding as another man chased him down. Everyone had seen this before. It was unlikely the two men were brothers by blood or by service. It was what one called the nameless afflicted—brother, sister, dear friend. Those treated by Os Vazios as children were elders now and still alive but not living. They were prone to wandering and were looked after and treated with reverence by Boorhians who passed down inherited guilt for having allowed Os Vazios onto the land in the first place. They were walking reminders of the danger of outsiders.

The man shouting "brother!" caught up with the wanderer and spoke gently to him, likely some offering of food, a bath, or shelter for the night, then wrapped his arm around his shoulders and led him away toward wherever home might be. The tavern patrons returned to their drinks, banging the cups twice on tabletops by way of salute before taking another swallow.

She startled as boisterous laughter disrupted the calm. A group of gruff workmen caked thick with the day's dirt and sweat laughed at a drunken compatriot who had managed to completely miss his stool on sitting down. He reached for a chain of lanterns to pull himself up again, but pulled them down in a crash instead. A small fire lit where the flames met spilled alcohol.

Daynja took advantage of the distraction and ducked into a dark alley beneath striped awnings. She waited, scanning the surrounding rooftops she could see. They would not be allowed to lose her. They would have to come looking. It was unlikely anyone had been given a kill order, so she wasn't too concerned with dying in the streets of her own city. But Negus needed to keep tabs on her until his move was ready to be made. She needed to know what that was. The tail would tell her.

Before long, she did notice something: someone was looking over the edge of the building beside her. A dark spot, their head perhaps, ruined the clean line of the building's shadow on the ground by popping into view and disappearing again. She kept her footfalls silent as she found and crept up the mud brick staircase to the third story roof.

Her face grew hot and her pulse quickened when she found Two standing on the far end, peering down into the tavern lights across the street, looking for her. She expected some no one, some faceless soldier who still had a name and pledged themselves to one of Negus's lackluster private guard. Two was arguably her favorite Shadow, with a well-rounded skillset and a whip-smart wit she felt mirrored her own. This felt like a betrayal.

"Smart, sticking to the rooftops here," Daynja called. She kept her senses tuned to any sign this was a trap. Two spun, surprise flickering across her pretty, dark face for only half a moment. "My hat reduced my vision to street level and made it obvious if I tried to look up. Plenty of time for you to hide or find your next vantage point. The moonlight gave you away, though. I guess I'm lucky you don't have your rifle."

Two said nothing, merely stood at attention and kept her eyes focused on nothing. She was unarmed and dressed as a civilian. The brass cuffs decorating her locs glinted in the moonlight.

"At ease," Daynja said. "Why are you following me?"

Two hesitated but looked her in the eye. "The Vice Minister, Xir. We have been ordered to watch you for signs of a threat."

"Signs of a threat? Since when do you take orders from anyone other than me?"

"His Imperial Majesty… Xir, they want the mask. *One* wants the mask."

"I thought he might." Daynja chuckled bitterly, staring down at the tavern where carousing had resumed. "And you? What do you want?"

"To do my job. And to be rewarded for it the way you have."

"I want that for you as well." Daynja nodded. If there was a way forward out of this, she'd want her to lead the future of the Shadow Army.

"I won't have a job as long as I follow you."

Daynja bristled as she started back to the stairs. She knew better than to feel wounded by her Shadows' ease of detachment. But still.

"You tell your brother he can have the mask when he retrieves it from me."

∴

The day of Daynja's deadline came quickly and night settled over Citadela without her turning over any plans to fulfill the mission in Eros. She'd spent the better part of two days making other preparations, cleaning the six steel barrels of Wadjet, her sniping rifle, spread like fingers over her dining room table, and braiding two kilometers of spiderwire into a loose mesh web from its compact, silver bundles of filigree. The idea was to set her trap in the Os Vazios monastery ruins well outside the city. A Shadow or two would come for the mask. She had to make sure *the army* came for her.

The fortress was still and silent. She was a finger into her two fingers of cachaça when dark spots flicked across the rooftops in her window. They converged in a moonless spot just beyond the War Room's rotunda on the edge of the drill pad. Six of them and the wooly white hair of the Chief Minister disappeared from view.

"About time." Daynja muttered. Frankly, she was finding this cloak-and-dagger business dull. There was much too much cloak and not nearly enough dagger.

She stood and stretched in the window, expecting a seventh shadow to dart around in the darkness. Rifle barrels fit into back slots on her vest of forty-nine knives. The spider-wire net went rolled into a neat parcel with the remaining spools into a bag on her hip, along with a leather bladder of the cachaça she hadn't drunk yet.

A deep breath before she locked her door behind her. She donned her mask again, and the black armor rose smooth as cooled magma to coat her skin. She stuck to the shadows and midnight paths to the Imperial Palace. Sentries were scant in the fortress. What with the damnable allegiance saturating every sinew and synapse of Citadela, there simply wasn't a reason to believe a threat would emerge.

Her steps were faint, save for the jostling of clay tiles on rooftops when she sped across them. The fiery alabaster dome of the palace loomed just ahead of her when she noticed a clattering of footfalls that weren't her own.

"General Édo," said an even voice behind her. It was Four. The girl's eyes were deep and black despite the moonlight pouring itself through everything else it touched. "Where are you off to?"

"The Hinterlands. Got a little homesick."

"With Wadjet?"

"*Huge* rats in the country," the General shrugged. She scanned the rooftops around them for more trouble. All was silent but the breeze. "So you're the one they didn't invite?"

"Someone's got to keep eyes on you. You've been erratic. We're concerned."

"You mean One is concerned."

"I mean we." Her hand moved to a holster on her hip, slowly. Casually. As if she knew the General wouldn't attempt to outdraw her. She carried two pistols, enviably gorgeous for the elaborate carvings in their handles. They'd been a gift, even though she lacked the vanity to appreciate the craftsmanship. Daynja remembered choosing Four for her marksmanship and her pragmatic, unflinching approach to her work. None of which bode well for at least one of them in this moment.

"Was it so easy for him to turn you all against me?" Daynja asked. Knowing they might have at least been conflicted about it would have been nice.

"We were always of Boorhia, General. *You* turned against *us*." Four replied.

So that was it, then. Daynja's hubris allowed her to hope the Shadows might —perhaps not love— honor her in some estimation close to the Empire. She'd been wrong.

"Fair enough," Daynja nodded. "I don't suppose you have capture, not kill orders, then."

"You have nothing more of value to Boorhia."

Well, damn.

Daynja frowned behind the mask, the unexpected ache of unrequited sentiment jabbing at her diaphragm. She breathed out. Her fingers twitched.

"But the mas*k*..." Four's *k* stuck in her throat where Daynja's blade caught it. A startle twinkled in Four's black eyes. She swallowed and blood like indigo ink began its trickle in the corners of her mouth. She sneered and managed to draw her gun anyway. Daynja fired another set of knives into the critical points of her assassin's arms, leaving them to hang limply at her sides. Four sank to her knees and the twinkle went out of her eyes before she toppled over onto the tiles.

Daynja stepped toward the body. A sense of loss buzzed about her head, irritating, like a mosquito in her periphery. Surely something needed to be said. Something offered. She knew somewhere within the smallest part of her that Four and the others didn't know any better.

The larger part of her, however, was furious. Daynja had made demigods of the little ingrates and been as much a mother figure to them as she or any of the Shadows had ever known. Without her, they'd still be toy soldiers, drowning in obscurity among the rest of the military's masses. She'd nurtured the spirited flames roiling in their guts and dragooned them into breathing fire. Yes, for Boorhia, but more so they could rise as she had. They *became* through her! And so did the Emperor.

Daynja huffed and left Four where she'd decided to die and took off again for Negus's quarters in the Imperial Palace. She'd just reached the black stone crown beneath the alabaster dome when a whistle sounded somewhere in the city. The two once-dulcet notes were now ominous precursors to a dangerous night.

She clung to the ornate coils of a column and peered out over city below. She couldn't see them, but she knew the other Shadows were coming.

She began to scale the dome for a proper vantage point. Her joints creaked their begrudging function. The shallow cracks she found in the stone barely fit her fingertips, and her booted feet scraped along its surface as she dragged herself upward.

With a final groan, she braced herself against the dome's ornate spire and assembled Wadjet from the barrels on her back and the stock on her hip. Where was One? She wanted One.

She scanned the rooftops again for any sign of movement, when she caught a glimmer of light as distant as the residential towers. It was unmistakably a scope mirror, but there was something else; gold flecks like the cuffs of locs.

"Who is that? Two—"

A sharp ping off Daynja's mask disoriented her for a moment and she crouched behind the spire. She inspected the mask to find a bullet, still warm and smoking, was lodged in its cheek. The armor underneath it hadn't even dented.

"Good shot, stupid girl," she leered.

If the General hoped to instill ambition in any of the Shadows, she hoped it would be Two.

But now the impressive little rat had shot her in the face.

Daynja put the mask back on and checked her sights for Two again, but the girl fired a second round, dinging off the dome near her foot. Furious, she resolved that there were still more pressing issues. But she would make sure there was time later to settle this.

Tethered to the spire, Daynja slid down the opposite end of the dome. A cadre of guards was mustering to get involved when she landed among them. Palace guards were the least useful guard bodies of Boorhia. If an invader made it this far, they'd be met with the very apologetic nieces, nephews, and siblings of established councilmembers, trained to spar, but never to win.

They were barely worth her attention. Daynja emptied the rest of Wadjet's rounds into the guards who wanted them the most. And when a few were still standing, she pulled a steel barrel from Wadjet and whipped them over the heads and backs with it until they stopped getting up.

Still using the gun barrel, Daynja broke a tall window into Negus's living chambers and stepped inside. More upholstered furniture than necessary was streaked with moonlight, but apart from that, darkness. It was comfortable, warm and dimly hazed with incense that smelled like sandalwood and whatever a merchant convinced him smelled of virility. Shouts outside announced the summoning of details to find the General or protect the Emperor.

Late, all of them. He was here, somewhere.

"Negus!" Daynja snarled, her heart pounding and back sore. She stretched and cracked those things that needed it. She barred the main chamber doors with one of Wadjet's barrels and slowly walked the adjoining rooms, flipping pillows and watching for changes in the light.

"Where are you, you dopey, pusillanimous bastard? I'm having a very bad night and I feel compelled to share it with you," she called.

A click behind her in the dark. She turned halfway around before Emperor Negus fired from a shaky hand. The bullet flattened against her armor and thudded to where it singed a hole in a very pretty rug.

"That's twice I've been shot tonight and it's starting to upset me." She grabbed his gun and tossed it aside. The Emperor backed himself into a chair where she circled him and began binding his wrists behind his back with a length of her spiderwire.

"They heard the gunshot. They know you're here." He sweat the words, panic fighting the contempt in his eyes. Daynja yanked and the knotted wire sliced like razors into his flesh. He screamed.

"Shh. I'll speak to them later. Right now I want to talk about you." She sat on the edge of a couch, reloading Wadjet and glancing at the windows to make sure they wouldn't be interrupted anytime soon.

"Your obsession with debt. Mine in particular. You see, anything I've owed the Empire for giving me a home, I paid to your mother. You've just reaped the benefits of my own ambition. I *gave* you all this," she gestured to the room around him, the guards in the hall, the land beyond every horizon outside his palace windows.

"You think of me as a pet, I know. But your throne is built on the bodies and nations *I* break. I made the Shadows you're using against me. The Three Known Worlds fear Boorhia's Imperial Warlord and her Shadow Army in their sleep. But whatever you have planned for the continued dulling of the world, I promise the Shadows won't be around to take part in it. The Eros girl will live, as will her feisty bunch, and I hope she finds whatever Old God is still lurking around here to take back everything else I've built beneath you."

"The world knows your mask. You are nothing without it. I—I gave you this power to be more than it! My mother gave you purpose!" He was all froth now, all anxiety and darting eyes. He wanted to scream, surely. But a scream might end the conversation too abruptly. And they both knew what waited at its end.

"You gave me a means to occupy myself. And now I have no further need of you," she smiled behind the cracked mask. "'*The Nation provides for the preservation of Our natural rights, among them to unmake the ones made by Our hand.*' Code of the Shadow Army. The thing we memorize as children. And so now remind me, Your Eminence, at the start of your unmaking," she stretched her palms before him, a black dagger in each, "whose hands made you?"

When he willed a sound like "you," Daynja jammed the daggers through either side of his neck and up through his cheeks making an X to keep his mouth shut. He would bleed out when they were removed. She looked at him and smiled before the clattering sounds of armored men outside the windows told her it was time to move again.

She unbarred the main doors and armed herself with Wadjet's barrels, whipping massed guards as she passed through them. But she would be overwhelmed soon and exits were limited.

She finally came upon an armory room with its lines of bulky gear and massive battle axes. At the far end was a barred window.

Guards funneled into the armory toward her. Daynja wondered if she would rip her own shoulders out, but began hammer throwing battle axes in close-set arcs toward her would-be captors, hurling left and then right and the left again as she moved backward. The hall was narrow and it didn't take long for bodies and shields to build up a blockage so she could fling an axe through the window. A hole shattered large enough for her to shimmy out and climb the stone down to a safe jumping distance.

She found herself in an alley and ran for all she was worth to the southern wall that led down to the city. Alarms in Citadela mingled with shouted reports that no one knew where she'd gone. Panic wouldn't besiege civilians for at least an hour. The remaining Shadows would find her before the regular troops screwed their heads on correctly.

Rain started and a clock chimed the eleventh hour. Daynja moved quickly through the alleyways and cobblestone streets. Much of the city was asleep save for cleaners, boisterous barflies and the occasional odd insomniacs peering out of bedroom windows in hopes of entertainment.

Daynja heard sloppy steps on a quiet street, accompanied by giggles and sharp "*hush*!" sounds. A pair of young lovers out well past bedtime spilled from an alleyway between a late-night coffee shop and a cobbler's. She ducked in the dark to breathe and wait for them to pass. Both were dressed for work, she with an apron, he with heavy gloves tucked into the back pocket of grease-spotted trousers. The girl carried her shoes in her hand.

They pulled each other into a space beneath an awning up the block and then pressed themselves together in a playful groping that said neither of them knew what to do next.

Daynja eyed the driftcycle the couple had left in the alleyway across the street. Steam rose from its cooling engine as the rain pelted its surface. It probably belonged to the boy judging by his boots. The amorous pair were sufficiently occupied, so Daynja darted across the street and walked the bike backward through the alley to start it up on the next block.

The main roads were empty. Anyone stumbling out of what passed for late-night debauchery here would slip home through the tavern-lined backstreets.

Daynja could make out the stone goddesses at the gate, their cascading locs and the leopard spots etched into their backs when the hum of new bikes forced her to check her corners. There hadn't been time to register much. Two bikes—loud sorts with tires—and a faint, two-note whistle. The intermittent sharp pop and gold spark of bullets fired and ricocheting off the cobblestones just inches on either side of her.

She accelerated and braced herself for something incoming. There was still a bomber unaccounted for, and the whistle had sounded a bit off —

In an instant of white-hot light and a concussive force that seemed to push the back of her ribs through their front, Daynja was airborne. The bike was blasted from beneath her.

Merda.

She was blind inside the mask. Her mind reeled to make sense of which way was down so she wouldn't land unkindly, but the ground faithfully rose to meet her anyway. Cobblestones fit poorly into the grooves of her body. Still, she was relieved to hit the street on her front and not her back where Wadjet would have broken her spine, armor or no.

Her vision cleared before the ringing in her ears and she lay panting, watching debris and chunks of road fall with the rain. Slightly, imperceptibly she flexed her fingers and her toes in her boots to make sure she could. She'd landed on one of her arms and the pain made her grind her teeth. And then she was still, straining through the pitch in her ears for when her mutinous Shadows would try to strip her of her mask.

Three was here. She had a chip in one of her front teeth from a training accident and it affected the notes of the Shadow whistle when she did it. The accident hadn't been her own carelessness, of course. It was a boy's fault. When Three also lost those three fingers in his poorly-controlled blast, the girl'd taken his arm with a hatchet as retribution.

She'd missed the target cut a few times. The boy didn't make it.

Two sets of footsteps rippled the rainwater pooling in the cracks around Daynja before the boots appeared on either side of her. She fingered the black blades she could reach on the front of her vest.

"Still smoldering. Good aim," said Five in an unreasonably jovial tone. He'd been one of Daynja's prized steel-wielding assassins and carried two black-bladed machetes on his back and a pistol on his hip.

Neither of them mattered, of course, because Daynja was a goddamned warlord.

"You going to run her through so we can get out of here?" Three sighed, the callous darling.

In a blurred instant, Daynja rolled and slashed the tendons in Five's ankles. He cried out and dropped to his knees, so the General didn't have to get to her feet to strip him of a blade and his sidearm. The former she used to remove his head. The latter put a bullet in Three's.

When Three fell, Daynja got to her feet with a groan.

Every bone and most of the tissue in her body protested violently, but she stifled herself when she heard another bike cut its engine. A rubble pile obscured her as long as she stayed crouched.

A small team of armed guards stood on the other side of the crater the bomb had created at the feet of the stone chimera goddess. They had heard the shot. Rather than wait for them to investigate, the General crawled back to Three's body, armed two blue bombs and lobbed them at the soldiers.

The explosions were separated by half a moment and then followed by the thunderous quake of a mountain cracking as the stone goddess broke into boulders and collapsed in the gateway.

Lights were coming on in the city and damp dust clouds billowed for blocks along the main road. The General quickly tucked what remained of Three's bombs into the spiderwire bag and used the cover of dust to flee through the space left by the monument. She didn't know if she'd killed them all. She only knew that no one followed her.

She crashed through sparse trees giving way to the dense forest outside the city's limits. Her sprint gave way to a march and then a trudge over tall grass and hidden rocks. All the while, her body screamed. The armor held together what was a tender and probably bruised bag of flesh. Keeping it active took a modest toll on her energy, but it had a way of refusing to leave her if she—if it—sensed danger. There were Shadows to wait for. Their mission was incomplete. If they hadn't completely abandoned their training, they would be upon her soon.

She plucked spiderwire from her bag and braided it absently as she walked. The path she took was overgrown now; the only steps ever on this route were probably hers. It ran along-side the main forest road and child-sized Édo had used it for her mischief and thievery back when she needed to. The main route would eventually cross the monastery ruins where she'd raised herself some kilometers into the forest.

If everyone really did know her story, they would know to look there for her.

A chill struck her spine. A couple of somethings were invisible in the trees around her. She sneered behind the mask. It was about time the twins showed up.

She drew two of Wadjet's barrels as Six and Seven launched themselves at her with their swords drawn. They fought like a whirlwind and Daynja was at its eye. Every move made by one was complemented by the other. There was a familiar rhythm to the flurry of clashing metal, and Daynja recalled years of watching the two of them spar. They were the only Shadows with any notion of defense.

That's the thing about being an assassin: almost all of it is stealth, the art of *not being* aside for the few moments spent as death's glorious incarnation. Combat means an assassin has failed to be invisible and Shadows rarely had reason for a fight. As twins, Six and Seven had always existed to one another, and they trained as foreseen and inevitable violence.

Daynja found that she was enjoying herself. "Faster!" The General barked, not taking advantage of the few kill windows she was offered. Instead, she rapped the boy's blade-wielding knuckles and whacked the girl high under her arm with a gun barrel. Seven checked that his hand wasn't broken and Six bellowed as she stumbled back. "You're small, Six. I shouldn't have access to your ribs."

The girl scowled, doubled over in the tall grass. Daynja turned her attention to the boy and addressed the cricks in her neck with audible pops. She was exhilarated. "Come on, Seven. You weren't sent here to dance. You mean to kill me."

The twins collected themselves. There was a nod between them, confirmation to each that the other was all right to go again. Daynja smiled. They advanced again with new tenacity.

"The mask! Get it off her!" Two's voice rang out, impatient and much more authoritative than Daynja had ever heard it. She was waiting in the trees with her rifle, invisible until her voice gave away her position.

"They may need an extra pair of hands," Daynja called, salivating at the idea of access to Two, the snake who bit her. "Swing down and help them out."

A pair of clipped buzzes shot beside Daynja's head. She ducked instinctively, but watched the life leave Six's eyes with the dark spray of an exit wound. Seven fell first, but Six's sword dropped to the grass before she went with it.

"No," Daynja panted over the twins' lifeless bodies bracketing her in the clearing. "NO!"

They were mine! She shrieked in her own head. Fury shook her so hard the world quaked around her. Spikes seemed to rise in the armor of her spine and the joints of her hands.

How *dare* she?

Two's rifle was being cocked again. "One will be here soon. I didn't have time for you to teach them how to kill you."

"Get down here, girl." The General snarled into the treetops, scanning them until she found the glint of gold cuffs in Two's locs.

"The mask, General. This can be over quickly."

"*I said get down here!*" She screamed, ferocious and guttural; a foreign sound that reminded her for a moment of Djinni. She whipped spiderwire rope, severing cleanly the branch on which Two crouched. She watched the girl crash to the ground, obscured by the grass and underbrush.

Something on the girl was clearly broken as she grimaced, scooting herself backward to the trunk of the tree. She raised her rifle and Daynja whipped the spiderwire again, cutting it in half.

The defiance in Two's eyes was insufficient. Daynja wanted terror.

She whipped the wire a third time, catching Two's ankle, and a fourth time, lassoing her torso. She wrapped the wire's length around her fist as she crossed to her traitor, cutting into Two's flesh slowly, methodically, with every tug.

"You miserable stain." Daynja growled. "What a disappointment you turned out to be."

"Likewise." Two groaned, a pained smirk playing on her lips. She had stopped squirming for the pain of the wire now grating into her bones, but she glared up into the General's face. "I almost had you…"

She choked on a laugh when Daynja slipped another loop of wire around her throat. The locs caught in it were severed and the knot of them dropped down over Two's face. A thin line of crimson began to appear as it tightened and she shut her eyes against the burning sensation of being slowly cut to pieces.

"Oh, Two. Is this how you imagined you'd die? An *almost* something?"

"You... everyt… to us once. Did you imag... you'd die Boorhia's Monster?"

What a pity the girl thought she would die clever.

"Look at me." Daynja tugged on the wire again and Two thrashed and grimaced before the panic of inevitable dismemberment finally took defiance's place in her eyes.

"Yes." She said. The General drew back fiercely on the spiderwire, and Two came apart in a squelch.

Rage sent Daynja crashing through the forest again, this time to pace in the main road, glowering at the northern darkness and the city she'd just escaped. Her boot prints were thick with the blood of Six or Seven or Two, or…

She waited there for One to appear with whatever legion he would bring to destroy her.

It would take a legion.

He hadn't materialized when the adrenaline began to subside. That niggling ache in the soft spot of her soul returned and threatened to crack the bones in her chest with its weight. A savage sort of anguish ripped through her in a howl. She clawed at the mask and stared at it with its little gold ring and the bullet like a mole lodged in its cheek. She wanted so badly to be rid of it, to crush it in her fist or throw it into the trees where it would rot in obscurity.

It stared back at her.

"Tough night?"

Reflexively, Daynja turned and flung a fist of knives at what turned out to be the Artful Djinni. They ducked and the blades nailed a tree trunk instead.

"Oh." Édo moaned. They were the kid again with the odd eyes, peering curiously at her from the edge of the road.

"A little high-strung. Maybe bring it down a little," Djinni frowned and plucked a blade out of the tree.

"I'm waiting for someone."

"From Citadela? I was just there. It'll be a bit. There's a huge mess and someone's gone and killed the Emperor. Wouldn't know anything about that, would you?" Djinni blinked, hands casually in the pockets of their dingy trousers.

Why, she *had* killed the Emperor, hadn't she? However fierce her grudge against her traitorous Shadows, she remembered that more was meant to come of this night. She tapped a fingernail pensively against the bullet in her mask, spit the last of her fury into the dust and sighed herself back to center.

"Want to help me with something, Djinni?" She asked with a final glare at the north.

"Thought you'd never ask," they replied with a grin.

∴

The Os Vazios monastery had been ruins already when Daynja was a child; and time hadn't stopped corrupting it when she left. Much of the roof she remembered sleeping under was on the ground, damp and covered in silt and vines. Remnants of stained glass windows crunched beneath her boots. Old porticos were just collapsing pillars. Signs she'd ever been here, ever existed before Citadela, were buried.

It was bright morning by the time she and Djinni arrived, caked in hours of dust and sweat. They'd been up the rest of the night lacing a long stretch of the main road with spiderwire netting and the rest of Three's bombs. Her armor fading meant she was in a place of relative safety.

She drank from the over-full stone well hidden in a jaboticaba grove behind the monastery. The air here was tart and floral, thick with the scent of the blackening fruit burdening the trees. The clean water pulled drying blood and clay from Daynja's hands and arms. She dropped the mask and her weapons, stripping to the mesh armor that wrapped her torso and dunked herself in the well. She was just as bruised as she thought she might be and her skin was marked with inky purple spots.

Djinni was sitting in a tree, slurping on a jaboticaba when she came up for air.

"So. Have you convinced yourself this is really about saving the Queen-Saint of Eros?"

"What else would it be about?" Daynja sputtered, using her shirt to towel off.

"You. What hasn't been about you yet?"

"I didn't make this about me." She gathered her things, climbing to a high wall remnant for the view. Her knuckles scraped climbing the stone without her armor. It was strange to see the power of her hands without it.

"No judgments here. I just want *you* to know that *I* know."

"Noted, Djinni." She slugged from her bladder of cachaça and peered through Wadjet's scope at Citadela glistening just short of the horizon. Nothing indicated they were mobilizing toward her. Not for now, anyway. One would come eventually and bring what remained of the might of the empire with him for what she'd done to Negus.

Daynja relaxed against the warming stone and took in the blue of the sky and enough cumulus clouds to threaten a storm if they wanted to. She ran her fingers along Wadjet's knicks and weathered spots and marveled at how it'd been largely undamaged in all this. Her eyes closed.

"They turned on me. All of them," she whispered to Djinni.

"They're Boorhian. Were they ever capable of being for you?"

"No." She pulled her mask over her face just enough to shade her eyes from the early afternoon sun. She had never been so tired. "Just as well. One will be here for the mask soon. I intend to give it to him. He's earned it."

"And then what?"

"You've been around long enough, Djinni. Infer."

"You versus the Boorhian Empire? You're much too calm for how human history dictates this will go." There was no hint of nervousness in their voice. They were silent awhile after, though, which Daynja found adorable on the edge of her well-deserved nap.

"It's funny," they said, finally. "If you were to do something like *die* on me, it'd be... well, I'd be disappointed."

Daynja laughed, a rich, life-giving sound that carried beyond the monastery and hopefully shook a soul someplace.

"Who loves me like you do, Djinni?"

∴

The sky was in its late violet sunset stage when she woke again. Djinni was gone. She bolted upright, her heart pounding with the sensation that she was late for something. Glimmers of light in a not-too-distant section of the main road caught her peripheral vision and she checked the scene through Wadjet's scope.

Leaves of trees rustled nearly as far as she could see. One had come bearing a squadron of souls for her.

Summoning what she could of her energy, Daynja tugged on her mask. She jumped from the wall where she'd been napping, but her knees weren't quick enough to settle and her legs gave way beneath her.

"Unbelievable," she groaned when, actually, it was perfectly believable. The wall would have been high even for someone half her age. There was a reason the men in the war council existed in an advisory capacity. But this was an inconvenient time to learn that lesson.

Alarm piqued her senses again but her armor was slow to generate. She could feel it bubbling in her blood, but it wouldn't surface. Had she donned it too long? Was her body still waking? *Of course,* she thought. The rest of her was slow to recover at her age. Why wouldn't magic blood armor take its own precious time?

She had to get to the monastery gates, but first came the wobbly stand and wary pressure testing of her mutinous legs. She determined the whole of Wadjet would be too much to carry now and she'd forgotten the vest that allowed her to carry it. Two barrels would be enough.

She managed to get to a weak jog, barrels in hand, and made her way to a flint line she'd arranged at the monastery gates. Her First Shadow was emerging at the top of the road with the front lines of the squadron he intended to use to persuade her to give up the mask.

Daynja snickered.

They came to a halt at the base of the ruined staircase. One looked impressed with himself. Columns of uniformed regulars stood at his back. The first line's guns were trained on her; and the lower halves of their faces were covered by unnecessary black sheaths. As if she cared about any of their identities.

She wouldn't manage to kill all of them. Just most of them.

One stood square and center, deadly battle chain wrapping his torso and piling around his thick neck like a heavy scarf. Busts of him would have looked good in this or that Hall of Great Whatevers the Empire would be erecting for as long as it existed. She wished she had the time or inclination to teach her Shadow that the smugness he tried to emulate was actually an earned thing. But that didn't matter just now either.

For now, she'd settle for conjuring that armor. She could manage, but the reveal would be much less poignant without it.

"Is this it?" He sneered. "Poetic setting for a last stand, but is it really just you and bits of Wadjet?"

"'Last stand?' Presumptuous," Daynja called back. The armor flickered in patches but didn't stay. "It took you this long to assemble this little party?"

"This is me formally notifying you that you've been relieved of duty. And if this is about that Eros girl, the Chief Minister will pursue her with forces under my command. So I am also informing you that you have saved nothing."

"Congratulations, Waahid. Though I'll admit I'm disappointed murdering children is so high on your list of aspirations."

"Whatever the Empire requires. I have always been Boorhia." He smiled darkly. "The mask, Daynja Édo."

It was an order. How sweet that she'd been there for his first.

Daynja shook her head, sad only for a moment that this was her legacy, and then resolved that this would also be the end of it.

She flung the mask at his feet and waited. He smirked as he picked it up, and she watched him brace for whatever he'd always imagined would happen when he put it on.

There was nothing.

Her smile spread with his confusion and the familiar slide of liquid stone stretched from her eyes over the rest of her body. She had never needed the mask.

"You're a shadow, One. There has only ever been me."

She brought Wadjet's barrels down against the flint line before her. A train of sparks sped along the spiderwire net beneath the army's feet. The tree line ignited. And then the bombs went off. The ground, the very air rumbled as waves of bodies careened against blasts of blue and white light. Daynja braced against the concussions, not wanting to lose sight of One as he coiled the chain around his fists.

"That's it, filho," Daynja muttered. "Get angry."

Soldiers searched frantically for cover. Mask or no, their steps faltered when finding the only way away from the flames was toward her.

She had no interest in them.

One was unfocused, his mind somewhere between self-preservation and the horror that came from the gross underestimation of an enemy. He'd never had a real, flesh opponent before. At least not one that could fight back.

She chuckled as he glared at her, the flame reflecting in his eyes. Too many of his troops were distracted with being on fire to heed his hollering.

He charged Daynja alone. The chain circled his forearms and whipped about him like violent tentacles, clipping his men indiscriminately as he carved his path. Daynja remembered teaching him to use it the way she used spiderwire: as an extension of the body only meant to bludgeon instead of snare his targets.

Normally, he was adept, but his anger made him reckless. It was the tired cliché that made Daynja prize Two over him.

She dodged and countered everything he threw at her, and let him scream his frustrations. She was, after all, in the middle of robbing him of everything.

The occasional explosion forced his balance. His footwork was sloppy on the stone steps and his swings were undisciplined. He inevitably tangled himself and Daynja decided they'd both had enough when the opportunity for barrel shots to his knees presented itself. She took it and peered down at him when he fell.

Her First Shadow hadn't been the shorter of them since he'd hit puberty. Wasn't that a lifetime ago?

She knew when her armor faded because embers on the evening air singed the fine hairs on her arms. One got to see her this way, without the mask and still greater than he had ever been.

"Is this it?" She shouted at him, panting in a mad grin. She swung her last bit of Wadjet hard enough to nearly knock One's head from his shoulders, and he spilled himself on the stone steps.

She looked out over the carnage as she'd done dozens of times before in Boorhia's name. The image of her maskless self was seared into the memories of the fleeing. It was the only time she could remember feeling there was a rightness to her mayhem.

She blinked. Her eyes shut just long enough for a searing heat to punch through her. At first she was startled. Her breath caught as she looked down to find she'd been shot. The neat, singed hole in her shirt just below the outer bend of her ribs began to leak. She pressed her hand to it, only to feel shockwaves of pain and a corresponding stickiness on her back.

Somewhat involuntarily, she dropped to the steps beside Waahid's body and looked out again for the soldier who meant to finish her. None seemed to notice. The shot was nowhere near center mast. A gun was more likely to have gone off in her general direction than having been aimed at her.

A mad sort of laugh escaped her as she tried to stand again but her legs would not allow it. All the years of violence and she'd never been shot before. All things considered, she could have gone another day without it. And now she'd die by accident.

"Oh, Waahid," she smiled wistfully. Tears of irony and excruciating pain escaped her eyes. "My absolute worst day and you still couldn't defeat me."

She was aware now of the pounding of her heart, the blood it was pumping inevitably out of her body. A breeze carried the scent of the jaboticaba with it to push out the thick scents of smoke and sweat. A few of the scattered soldiers noticed her sitting on the steps and she was sure something about her face indicated it wasn't of her own volition. They pointed their weapons somewhat boldly as they crept closer. Daynja's defense impulse was tempered by the loud grinding of her bones as they'd resigned themselves to rest.

The mission was accomplished. It might be nice to die here after all.

A shadow launched itself from over her head and Daynja cleared the blur in her eyes to find she was staring at the back of Djinni as the loc-haired kid. They spread their arms wide before crashing them together in a clap that emanated broad, whistling waves of wind. The nearest trees bent under the force and anguished screams rang out as the remaining soldiers fell to their knees cradling their heads for their destroyed eardrums.

"What are you doing?" Daynja groaned.

"What are *you* doing? Get up!" Djinni snapped.

Daynja roared as she fought herself to lean forward. "I'm shot."

Djinni shoved her aside to gruffly inspect her. "It went in and out, you big baby! We can't patch you up here so get up."

"Why are you here? I didn't ask for your help," Daynja huffed, using one of Wadjet's barrels to stand herself into some semblance of upright.

"You don't thank me either," Djinni said, then nodded at where Waahid lay on the steps. "I see you squared things with One."

Daynja said nothing. Very little was square. She'd destroyed the monsters she created and was surviving them all. He had still been her first Shadow.

Djinni let her prop herself against their shoulder and reached around to press against the wound in her back. She cursed behind clenched teeth. Together, they limped back into the jungle.

"Where are we going?" Daynja asked.

"First day of the rest of your life? Anywhere," Djinni said cheerily. " You know, I spoil you."

L.D. Lewis is a coffee enthusiast and writer of SFF. She also serves as Art Director for FIYAH Literary Magazine for Black Speculative Fiction. She lives in Florida, on deadline, and under the judgmental gaze of her cat, Gustavo. Tweet her @ellethevillain